1

5

VROOOM

MISSED THE BUS?

HUH?

HOOOWWLL

WHAT'S THAT?!

WHAT'S *HE* DOING?

CHECK IT OUT! A *DODGEBALL!*

YEAH, THEY TAKE IT SERIOUSLY AROUND HERE. YOU PLAY?

UH, NO, I MEAN, *YEAH.*

BACK AT MY OLD SCHOOL, I WAS A *DODGEBALL LEGEND.* I WAS ALL-STATE, FIRST TEAM.

LUCKY YOU. I HATE DODGEBALL.

YOU DO?

IT'S PROBABLY HARD FOR YOU TO UNDERSTAND, BUT *NOT EVERYBODY* IS GOOD AT DODGEBALL.

UM, ACTUALLY, I WAS . . .

C'MON, THE COAST IS CLEAR, LET'S GET IN BEFORE *THE HORDE* SEES US.

THE HORDE? WHAT'S A *HORDE?*

15

PLEASE, OH, PLEASE, MRS. DAGGER, *WISE AND POWERFUL QUEEN* OF THE SCHOOL. I BEG YOU. PLEASE, I'LL NEVER DO IT AGAIN!

STOP GROVELING, MR. KOZLOWSKI. YOU'RE GETTING SPITTLE ON MY SHOES!

YOU KNOW THE RULES. *NO* ELECTRONIC DEVICES ON SCHOOL GROUNDS. THANK YOU FOR YOUR *DONATION!*

BUT IT'S NOT MINE! IT'S MY BROTHER'S!

TOO BAD.

THAT STINKS!

PERHAPS, YOU'D LIKE TO FAMILIARIZE YOURSELF WITH THIS DURING LUNCH PERIOD DETENTION.

Camelot Middle School Rules and Regulations Vol. IX

RULES ARE RULES, MR. KOZLOWSKI. IF WE DIDN'T HAVE RULES, DO YOU KNOW WHAT WE'D HAVE?

FUN?

NOBODY MESSES WITH . . .

JOSEPH ROMAN, WHAT'S GOING ON HERE?

HULLO, MRS. DAGGER.

I'M *SURPRISED* AT YOU, YOUNG MAN.

SORRY, MRS. DAGGER.

YOU SHOULD KNOW BETTER.

WHY AREN'T YOU BOYS PRACTICING DODGEBALL?

I WANT YOU TO WIN THE DISTRICT TROPHY AGAIN.

HANNIBAL?

I HAVE A VERY GOOD FEELING ABOUT THIS SEASON.

NO LONGER SHALL WE CRAWL IN THE LOWER DIVISIONS.

NO SIR, THIS TIME, *VICTORY* IS WITHIN OUR GRASP.

THIS YEAR THE MIGHTY WILL FALL . . .

AAAA

HHHHH

YOU! IN MY OFFICE. *NOW!*

28

YOU WANT ME TO *STEAL* IT??

SSHHHH! IT'S NOT STEALING! IT'S MORE LIKE *RETRIEVING.*

WHEN YOU GET IN THERE, I'LL GIVE YOU THE SIGNAL. JUST GRAB IT.

WHAT SIGNAL?

I KNEW I COULD COUNT ON YOU. LATER!

PIZZA PALA

UH! WAIT! WHERE ARE YOU GOING?

WHERE IS *WHO GOING?*

29

AND WHO ARE *YOU!?* WHAT EDUCATIONAL BLACK HOLE SPIT YOU OUT AND BLESSED US WITH YOUR *WORMLIKE* PRESENCE?

MY NAME IS ARTHUR KING. I JUST MOVED FROM CORNWALL. I'M NEW.

YEAH. HOORAH. WONDERFUL. WE CERTAINLY ARE *LUCKY* HERE. LET'S SEE WHAT YOUR FILE SAYS.

HMMF, I SEE, YOU MUST BE SOOOO PROUD OF YOURSELF. *B-MINUS. B-MINUS. C-PLUS.* TELL ME, MR. KING, ARE YOU GOOD AT ANYTHING?

WELL, I'M . . .

THAT'S NOT A QUESTION. *≥SIGH≤*

I DON'T KNOW HOW THEY DO THINGS OVER IN CORNWALL, BUT AT CAMELOT MIDDLE SCHOOL, WE OPERATE ON ONLY THE *HIGHEST* OF STANDARDS.

WE DO NOT TOLERATE CONNIVING LITTLE *WORMS* THAT GO AROUND SUBVERTING THE EDUCATIONAL PROGRAM AND ASSAULTING OUR FACULTY.

I'M SORRY, BUT IT WAS AN ACCIDENT.

WHAT ARE YOU STILL DOING HERE?

UH, I DON'T HAVE A LOCKER YET, MA'AM.

A LOCKER, YOU SAY? *MISS FLUNKE,* WE MUST GIVE THIS FINE BOY A LOCKER!

MMM, THIS IS REALLY GOOD PIZZA. YOU SHOULD . . .

MISS FLUNKE, GIVE MR. KING LOCKER *#001XCL.*

YES, MA'AM, UH, THAT LOCKER IS . . .

IT HASN'T BEEN OPENED IN YEARS.

DON'T BE SILLY. GIVE MR. KING LOCKER #001XCL.

BUT . . .

GLADYS . . . GIVE . . . HIM . . . THE . . . LOCKER!

YES, MA'AM.

I WILL BE KEEPING AN EYE ON YOU, WORM. I KNOW WHAT YOU'RE UP TO. TWO MORE STRIKES, AND YOU'RE OUT. *TWO MORE.*

34

38

I DON'T . . . ?

THAT'S THE *BUSTED* LOCKER I SHOWED YOU THAT NOBODY CAN OPEN. THE ONE WITH THE RHYMING GRAFFITI ON IT.

I HEARD IT'S *CURSED*. THIS KID, TERRY WHITE, HAD THAT LOCKER. HE TRIED TO OPEN IT. AND THAT WAS THE LAST ANYBODY EVER SAW HIM. I THINK IT'S A *DIMENSIONAL PORTAL* TO A BARREN WASTELAND.

TERRY MOVED TO NEW JERSEY.

WHATEVER.

THIS IS *TOO COOL!* WAIT TILL EVERYONE FINDS OUT!

NO, DON'T! IT'S JUST A STUPID LOCKER.

BUT IF YOU OPEN IT, YOU'LL *RULE* THE SCHOOL.

JOIN FUTURE LEADERS

LOST

AND IF I CAN'T?

THEN YOU'LL CARRY YOUR BOOKS AROUND ALL YEAR.

WHAT'S YOUR NEXT CLASS?

SCIENCE WITH . . .

THE MAIN OFFICE. I'M ALSO YOUR FACULTY ADVISOR. WHAT TOOK YOU SO LONG?

I GOT LOST. THERE WERE THESE THREE . . .

OH, YOU MET THE LADIES OF THE LUNCH.

YEAH, THEY'RE KIND OF . . .

WEIRD? RIGHT. HAIRNETS ARE TOO TIGHT, IF YOU ASK ME. THEY SAY THEY SEE THE FUTURE BY READING THE LUNCH MENU.

LIKE TODAY FOR INSTANCE: CHICKEN PATTY AND MACAROONS.

BE FOREWARNED, A BATTLE LOOMS.

LUNCH

REALLY? I'M GLAD I BROUGHT MY LUNCH. NOW WHERE WAS I?

RAAWK! POP QUIZ!

THANK YOU, OBERON.

QUIZ

I DID TELL YOU YOU'D BE TESTED.

41

DANGER! *RAAWK!*

KNOCK, KNOCK

MR. MERLYN.

IS THIS A DAGGER I SEE BEFORE ME?

MAY I SPEAK TO YOU FOR A MOMENT? IN *PRIVATE*.

YES, OF COURSE. BUT, I WANT YOU TO KNOW I HAD NO IDEA ABOUT THE PIZZAS.

MR. MERLYN, YOU'VE BEEN HERE EIGHT YEARS.

NINE, I'VE BEEN HERE *NINE* YEARS.

WHATEVER. WHAT I'M TRYING TO SAY IS, DON'T YOU THINK A MAN OF YOUR *UNIQUE* ABILITIES WOULD BE MUCH BETTER SERVED AT ANOTHER SCHOOL? *A SCHOOL FAR, FAR AWAY.* IN ANOTHER DISTRICT.

I GET YOUR POINT. YOU WANT TO GET *RID* OF ME.

NO.

YES.

43

HEY, GUYS!

DID YOU TELL *EVERYBODY?*

NOOO. NOT *EVERYBODY.* JUST A COUPLE KIDS IN THE LIBRARY, A FEW IN GYM CLASS AND A HANDFUL IN STUDY HALL.

OPEN IT!

YEAH!

WE WANNA SEE THE *SKELETON!*

WHAT DO I *DO?*

TRY TO OPEN IT. IT'S YOUR LOCKER.

IF YOUR HEART BE TRUE AND FINE, TURN THE DIAL LEFT TO 9.

27 TO THE RIGHT, GIVES THE OWNER STRENGTH AND MIGHT.

LEFT AGAIN TO NUMBER 3, A KING TO ALL THE STUDENTS BE.

OK.

DON'T TOUCH THAT LOCKER!

IF YOUR HEART BE TRUE AND FINE,

TURN THE DIAL LEFT TO NINE.

TWENTY-SEVEN TO THE RIGHT,

001 XCL

GIVES THE OWNER STRENGTH AND MIGHT.

LEFT AGAIN TO NUMBER THREE,

A *KING* TO ALL THE STUDENTS BE.

IF ANYONE THINKS THEY CAN BEAT ME, *STEP RIGHT UP!*

AS FOR YOU, YOU THINK YOU'RE *FUNNY?* THINK YOU CAN MAKE ME LOOK *STUPID?* I'M GONNA *BOUNCE* YOU LIKE A DODGEBALL.

NOBODY MESSES WITH *JOE ROMAN.*

WAIT! LET HIM GO! LET'S SETTLE THIS A DIFFERENT WAY. HOW ABOUT DODGEBALL? OUR TEAM AGAINST *THE HORDE.*

WHAT DID YOU DO *THAT* FOR?

I SAVED YOUR LIFE. BESIDES, YOU'RE A *DODGEBALL LEGEND*, RIGHT? YOU WERE ALL-STATE, FIRST TEAM.

YOU WERE *ALL-STATE?* IS THAT GOOD?

FINALLY, WE'RE GONNA GET EVEN WITH THE HORDE!

LISTEN, ACTUALLY I WAS . . .

DUDE, I'M *STARVING*.

WE'LL HAVE TIME TO DISCUSS THIS AT LUNCH.

LUNCH, THAT'S RIGHT, I DON'T HAVE ONE.

WHAT'S THIS?

WHERE'D *THIS* COME FROM?

NO, I MEAN THE DODGEBALL GAME.

ARTIE, FOR YEARS THE HORDE HAS BEEN *PUSHING* US AROUND. THEN YOU SHOW UP AND EVERYTHING CHANGES. WE'VE BEEN WAITING FOR SOMEONE LIKE YOU. WE CAN *BEAT* THEM. I KNOW IT.

BUT I'M JUST...

YOU'RE LIKE THAT CHOSEN ONE GUY. YOU MADE JOE EAT SOAP, YOU TRIPPED DAGGER, YOU GOT MY GAME BOY BACK AND YOU OPENED THE CURSED LOCKER.

YOU, MY FRIEND, ARE THE CHOSEN ONE, THE LEGEND.

I'M NOT THE CHOSEN ONE! I'M USUALLY *THE LAST CHOSEN ONE!*

WHAT DO *YOU* THINK, MR. MERLYN?

SORRY I HAD TO WORK LATE, KIDS. HOW WAS YOUR FIRST DAY?

GREAT, MOM! I'VE ALREADY GOT *CHEERLEADING* TRYOUTS TODAY.

THAT'S *TERRIFIC*, MORGAN. WHAT ABOUT YOU, ARTIE?

I DON'T LIKE CHEERLEADING.

HA HA VERY FUNNY, YOU KNOW WHAT I MEANT.

ARTIE'S PLAYING IN A BIG *DODGEBALL* GAME ON FRIDAY!

IS THIS TRUE? THIS FRIDAY? I'LL BE THERE.

I'M *SOOO* PROUD OF YOU. JUMPING RIGHT BACK ON THE HORSE.

I'LL SEE YOU TONIGHT. GOOD LUCK WITH THE TRYOUTS, MORGAN.

THANKS, MOM. BYE-BYE.

WARTIE, WHAT ARE YOU DOING?

Valiant Flakes

TRYING TO EAT MY CEREAL.

NO, I MEAN TELLING EVERYONE YOU'RE A DODGEBALL STAR. *AS IF!*

I BETTER GET MY DIARY BACK BECAUSE IF I DON'T?

MORGAN

I'M GONNA TELL *ALL* YOUR LITTLE FRIENDS THAT YOU'RE REALLY A DODGEBALL *LOSER.*

MORGAN

UH . . . WHAT'S THIS?

MISSING TARANTULA

SWEET! YOU MADE POSTERS? THANKS!

I DIDN'T MAKE THEM. I FOUND THEM, IN THE LOCKER.

UH-HUH.

YEAH, RIGHT.

THIS LOCKER? THE MAGIC SANDWICH LOCKER?

ANYWAYS, WAYNE AND I THINK IT WOULD BE A GOOD IDEA IF WE HAD A DODGEBALL PRACTICE.

PRACTICE!?

I KNOW, *YOU* DON'T NEED IT. BUT *WE* DO.

YEAH, BUT...

BESIDES, MAYBE YOU CAN TEACH US A FEW MOVES.

OK, BUT...

COOL! I'LL TELL WAYNE! THANKS AGAIN FOR THE POSTERS. I'LL GO HANG THEM UP!

AW, FISH STICKS, I'M *DOOMED*.

ARE YOU OK?

RAWWK! HAIL TO THE KING!

MR. MERLYN?

WHAT CAN I DO FOR YOU, ARTHUR?

YOU KNOW I HAVE THIS LOCKER?

YES I KNOW. *#001XCL.* IT HASN'T BEEN OPENED IN YEARS. THAT'S QUITE A *CROWNING* ACHIEVEMENT.

THAT'S WHAT I HEAR. ANYWAYS, I'VE BEEN FINDING *STUFF* IN IT. STUFF THAT WASN'T THERE BEFORE.

WHAT KIND OF STUFF? *SKELETONS?* STACKS OF MONEY? DIMENSIONAL PORTALS?

NO. BORING STUFF, LIKE BALONEY SANDWICHES AND POSTERS. DO YOU THINK IT'S *MAGIC?*

HMM, NOTHING VERY *MAGICAL* ABOUT A BALONEY SANDWICH. ALTHOUGH MY AUNT BESSIE WOULD GRILL THE BALONEY FIRST AND MMM, MMM, THAT WAS PRETTY MAGICAL.

BUT THAT'S NOT WHAT YOU WANTED TO HEAR ABOUT, IS IT?

AH, NO.

BEING A SCIENCE GUY AND ALL, I DON'T KNOW MUCH ABOUT MAGIC.

BUT I CAN TELL YOU THAT IF THIS LOCKER IS LIKE MOST THINGS IN THIS WORLD, YOU'LL GET AS MUCH OUT OF IT AS YOU PUT INTO IT.

OH, OK. I WAS HOPING FOR THOSE DIMENSIONAL PORTALS OR STACKS OF MONEY.

AREN'T WE ALL, ARTHUR, AREN'T WE ALL?

AFTER SCHOOL

SO, WHERE IS HE?

HE SAID HE'D BE HERE. HE'LL BE HERE.

SORRY, I'M LATE. MRS. DAGGER MADE ME CLEAN UP ALL THOSE RIPPED POSTERS.

I THINK I SAW *HANNIBAL*.

WHAT? WHERE?

HE WAS IN MY LOCKER. BUT WHEN I LOOKED AGAIN HE WAS GONE.

TOLD YOU, DIMENSIONAL PORTAL.

YOU KNOW THAT GIRL GWEN?

GWENDOLYN LEE? WHY, YOU LIKE HER?

NO! SHE SAYS OUR TEAM NEEDS A NAME.

THAT'S NOT A BAD IDEA.

YEAH! HOW ABOUT *THE DECAPITATORS!*

73

74

75

SHE'S A *GIRL*. IT'S A KNOWN FACT, GIRLS *CAN'T PLAY* DODGEBALL.

AND YET YOU'RE A *MORON*, BUT WE LET YOU PLAY.

GWEN HAS A POINT. WE NEED A *FOURTH*.

NO PROBLEM, I GOT AN IDEA!

THIS CAN'T BE GOOD.

IN A VIDEO GAME, WHEN YOU'RE *STUCK*, WHAT DO YOU DO?

GET THE CHEAT CODE?

THIS IS TRUE. BUT WHAT IF YOU CAN'T FIND THE CHEAT CODE? YOU *HIRE* A MERCENARY.

A *DODGEBALL MERCENARY?*

HERE WE GO.

YOU KNOW ONE?

YES, WE GET *SCOTT SAVAGE*. MY BROTHER IS FRIENDS WITH HIM.

78

I'M NOT SURE I KNOW WHAT YOU ARE TALKING ABOUT, MR. MERLYN.

I'M TALKING ABOUT A *LITTLE WAGER*. ARE YOU AWARE OF A CERTAIN DODGEBALL GAME ON FRIDAY BETWEEN THESE BOYS AND ANOTHER GROUP, JOE'S HORDE?

DODGEBALL? YES, HMMM. YOU SAY THESE THREE AGAINST THE HORDE? PLEASE, TELL ME MORE.

IF *THE HORDE* WINS, INSTEAD OF THESE GUYS GETTING EXPELLED, *I'LL QUIT.*

REALLY? MY, MY, THAT IS TEMPTING. AND IF THEY SHOULD SOMEHOW WIN?

ARTHUR, WAYNE, PERCY AND I STAY, AND YOU MUST WEAR A *GORILLA SUIT* TO SCHOOL.

DEAL! I'LL HAVE THE EXIT PAPERS READY FOR YOU TO SIGN.

I'LL RENT THE GORILLA SUIT.

AFTER SCHOOL

I HOPE THERE'S SOMETHING TO *EAT* IN HERE, I'M STARVING.

ALRIGHT!

GEE, THANKS.

YOU READY?

I GUESS SO.

SO, WHERE DO WE FIND THIS SCOTT KID?

DUDE, HE RULES *ARCADIA.*

NO FIGHTING IN ARCADIA.

SORRY, ANGUS. I WAS JUST LEAVING.

I AM *THE GAMEKEEPER.*

YOUR FRIEND TELLS ME YOU WISH TO SEE SCOTT.

YES, WE'D LIKE TO . . .

THERE IS ONLY ONE WAY TO SEE SCOTT. YOU FIRST *DEFEAT* HIS CHAMPION.

WHO'S THAT?

ME.

DEFEAT YOU? I THOUGHT THERE WAS NO FIGHTING IN . . .

NOT FIGHTING. YOU MUST *BEST ME* IN MY FAVORITE GAME.

SAVAGE BLADES.

SAVAGE BLADES

INSERT COINS

NO, YOU CAN'T FIT IN *HERE*, BUT I BET YOU'LL FIT OVER *THERE*.

DOWN THE RAVINE YOU WILL FIND A CULVERT. IT'S BARRED BUT I THINK YOU ARE SMALL ENOUGH TO FIT THROUGH.

GO IN THERE AND BRING BACK MY FATHER'S KNIFE, AND I'LL DEFEAT THE HORDE SINGLE-HANDEDLY. YOU HAVE MY WORD.

NOW I KNOW WHERE WE ARE. WE'RE NEAR . . .

HOOOWWLL

THE *BEAST!*

THERE IT IS!

GOT IT!

HOOW...LL

HUH?

WHOA!

AAHHHHHH!

ARTIE, WHERE HAVE YOU BEEN? ARE YOU ALL RIGHT? WHAT IS *THAT?*

I'M OK, I JUST FELL DOWN.

HIS NAME IS *BEAST.* I RESCUED HIM. CAN WE KEEP HIM?

EWW! NO WAY AM I SHARING THE HOUSE WITH ANOTHER *FILTHY ANIMAL.*

MORGAN, BE NICE.

IT'S NOT FAIR! HOW CAN YOU LET HIM HAVE A DOG WHEN HE STEALS MY THINGS?

I DON'T HAVE YOUR *DUMB* DIARY!

LIAR!

SO, CAN WE KEEP HIM?

A DOG IS A LOT OF RESPONSIBILITY.

108

109

SECRET SECRETARY TO QUEEN MEANIE, THE OWL HAS LEFT THE NEST. OVER.

MISS FLUNKE? IS THAT YOU?

ROGER, I THOUGHT WE OUGHT TO USE CODE NAMES. OVER.

OF COURSE YOU DID. WHAT'S GOING ON?

THE OWL IS LEAVING. OVER.

EXCELLENT, YOU KNOW WHAT TO DO.

ROGER THAT. OVER AND OUT.

YOU SEEN SCOTT YET?

IT'S ALMOST FOUR.

DUDE, HE SAID HE'D BE HERE.

YO! ARTIE!

ANGUS, AM I EVER GLAD YOU GUYS ARE HERE.

WHERE'S SCOTT?

SCOTT CAN'T MAKE IT. HE'S GROUNDED. HIS FATHER FOUND OUT HE TOOK THE KNIFE. HE SAYS HE'S SORRY.

I KNEW IT!

BUT SCOTT TOLD ME TO GIVE YOU A TOKEN OF HIS GRATITUDE. HE SAYS YOU ARE ALWAYS WELCOME IN ARCADIA.

GEE, THANKS.

WHAT IS IT?

A TOKEN.

arcadia Land of Fun

114

WHAT HAS HAPPENED TO MR. MERLYN?

WHY DID WE GET THE *GIRLS' LOCKER* ROOM?

I BET MRS. DAGGER IS BEHIND THIS.

HELLO, GENTLEMEN. THE GAME STARTS IN FIFTEEN MINUTES. YOU KNOW THAT IF YOU DO NOT HAVE FOUR PLAYERS YOU WILL HAVE TO FORFEIT.

YOU ALSO WILL NEED *GYM CLOTHES,* WHICH I SEE YOU HAVE.

WHAT ABOUT MR. MERLYN?

IF HE'S NOT HERE IN TIME, WE'LL START WITHOUT HIM. HE'S PROBABLY SEEN YOUR CHANCES AND HAS ALREADY DECIDED TO LEAVE.

WE'RE SO DEAD. WE'RE *DEADER* THAN DEAD.

WE WOULDN'T BE IF IT WASN'T FOR YOU AND YOUR *STUPID* GAME BOY!

HEY, YOU'RE THE JERK WHO *CHALLENGED* THE HORDE IN THE FIRST PLACE.

ME? WHAT ABOUT THAT DUMB TRIP TO ARCADIA?

WE GOT SCOTT TO HELP US.

WHERE IS HE NOW?

AT LEAST I'M DOING SOMETHING! YOU JUST . . .

STOP! IT'S NOT YOUR FAULT! IT'S MY FAULT.

NO IT'S NOT. YOU'RE OUR ONLY CHANCE AT WINNING.

YOU'RE THE DODGEBALL LEGEND.

NO I'M NOT!

QUIT? ARE YOU KIDDING?

AFTER ALL WE'VE BEEN THROUGH?

NO WAY! YOU MAY STINK AT DODGEBALL, BUT WE'RE IN THIS TOGETHER. BESIDES, YOU'RE STILL THE *CHOSEN GUY* WITH THE LOCKER.

AS MUCH AS I HATE TO SAY IT, HE'S RIGHT. YOU'RE THE CHOSEN GUY.

THANKS, GUYS.

WE STILL DON'T HAVE A FOURTH PLAYER.

THERE'S GWEN?

UH-UH, I DON'T WANT . . .

GET OVER IT! SHE MAY NOT BE THE PLAYER *YOU WANT.* BUT SHE'S THE PLAYER *WE NEED!*

WHAT DID YOU SAY?

I SAID...

NEVER MIND. WAYNE, GO BEG GWEN TO PLAY FOR OUR TEAM.

NO! NEVER!

I...OK.

PERCY, GO LOOK FOR MR. MERLYN.

WHERE ARE YOU GOING?

I LEFT SOMETHING IN MY LOCKER.

WHAT DO YOU WANT ME TO DO WITH HIS BIKE? OVER.

LEAVE IT. GET BACK HERE AS SOON AS YOU CAN.

001XCL

HEY THERE.

GREAT CATCH BY GWEN LEE! HORDEMAN STEWART MONK IS *OUT!*

OH, THAT HURT. DWAYNE FERRYMAN IS OUT! THE HORDE ONLY HAS TWO PLAYERS LEFT.

ARTHUR KING IS BACK *IN.*

OOH, NOT SO FAST!

THE HORDE IS TEAMING UP ON GWEN NOW. IT DOESN'T LOOK GOOD FOR THE KNIGHTS.

STAY BEHIND ME. MOVE WHEN I MOVE.

NOW!

WAYNE KOZLOWSKI HAS BEEN HIT IN THE HEAD. JOE ROMAN SHOULD BE OUT.

HEY! HE HIT ME IN THE HEAD.

DON'T BE A CRYBABY.

UNBELIEVABLE! THE REF IS CALLING KOZLOWSKI OUT! GWEN LEE IS LEFT THERE ALONE. WHAT ARE THE KNIGHTS GOING TO DO?

Knights
PLUMBING & HEATING

MONDAY

WHAT ARE YOU *LAUGHING* AT?

HEE-HEE-HEE-HEE-HEE-HEE

STOP LAUGHING!

DETENTION FOR YOU!

AND YOU . . .

AND YOU . . .

YOU . . .

AND YOU . . .

WHO WANTS TO PLAY DODGEBALL?

Dodgeball legend Frank Cammuso is a three-time recipient of the Wedgie. He has also received the prestigious Noogie and the Hurtz Donut.

Cammuso is the Eisner-nominated creator of the Max Hamm, Fairy Tale Detective graphic novels. He draws political cartoons for *The Post-Standard* and his work has appeared in *Newsweek*, *The New York Times*, *The Washington Post*, and *USA Today*. He lives with his wife in Syracuse, New York.

This book is for anyone who has ever been picked last.
— FC

Special thanks to Ngoc Huynh, Hart Seely,
Phil McAndrew, Peter Allen, Tom Peyer, Michael Cho,
Bruce Coville, Michael and Harrison Jantze, Sheila
Keenan, Phil Falco, Janna Morishima, David Saylor, David
McCormick, all the fine folks at *The Post-Standard*
and especially the students, faculty, and staff of
Durgee Junior High School.

All rights reserved. Published by Graphix, an imprint of Scholastic Inc., *Publishers since 1920*.
SCHOLASTIC, GRAPHIX, and associated logos are trademarks and/or registered trademarks of
Scholastic Inc.

Library of Congress Cataloging-in-Publication Data

Cammuso, Frank.
The dodgeball chronicles / by Frank Cammuso. — 1st ed.
p. cm. — (Knights of the lunch table ; 1)
ISBN 978-0-439-90322-6 (alk. paper)
1. Graphic novel. I. Title.
PN6727.C28D63 2008
741.5'973—dc22
2007037480

26 25 24 23 22   16 17 18 19 20/0

First edition, July 2008

Edited by Sheila Keenan
Creative Director: David Saylor
Book design by Phil Falco
Lettering by John Green
Printed in China   38

KNIGHTS OF THE LUNCH TABLE

THE DODGEBALL CHRONICLES

by

FRANK CAMMUSO

AN IMPRINT OF

◼SCHOLASTIC

New York Toronto London Auckland Sydney Mexico City New Delhi Hong Kong Buenos Aires